Livicated to the memory of David Floyd De Souza and my mum,
Eileen who continues to be a great source of strength to me.
MDS

Livicated to Monica, Melodie, John and Al
with love and thanks
GW

And a very special thank you to our technical
advisor: Isaac Muscatt

First published 2003 by Little Roots
This edition published 2012 by Macmillan Children's Books
a division of Macmillan Publishers Limited
20 New Wharf Road, London N1 9RR
Basingstoke and Oxford
Associated companies throughout the world
www.panmacmillan.com

ISBN: 978-1-4472-1696-4

3 5 7 9 8 6 4 2

A CIP catalogue record for this book is available from the British Library.

Printed in China

Rastamouse

and

Da Bag-a Bling

Words by

Michael De Souza & Genevieve Webster

Pictures by

Genevieve Webster

MACMILLAN CHILDREN'S BOOKS

Here's Rastamouse, Scratchy and Zoomer,
Also known as the Easy Crew,
Crime-fighting, special agents,
And a red-hot reggae band too.

Speeding through the darkness,
By the light of a luminous moon,
They're off to 'Nuff Song' studio,
To record their latest tune.

But across the road and through the woods
On the other side of town,
The orphans are getting out of bed
When they should be settling down.

Those babies should be fast asleep,
Instead they're in a trance.
Moving to an irie beat
That makes them want to dance.

Bandulu, chef at the orphanage,
Is up late and baking a pie,
So he doesn't hear the orphans wake
Or see them dancing by.

Meanwhile back at the studio,
The crew are in a fix.
"Dis tune is sounding crucial,
But someting missing from da mix."

NUFF ♪ SONG

And as they start to play it back,
This is what they hear:
An emergency transmission
Through the radio loud and clear.

"RASTAMOUSE!
COME IN! COME IN!
ARE YOU READING ME?
MESSAGE FROM PRESIDENT WENSLEY DALE,
COME IMMEDIATELY!"

So they kick out from the studio
With Rastamouse up front,
Who busts an awesome ollie grind
And a double flip-side stunt.

Scratchy turns a misty flip,
As Zoomer zooms along,
And soon they're at the President's
To ask him what is wrong.

Wensley Dale says, "Tings is rough,
Me want you all to listen.
Me get a call from de orphanage,
Dem baby mice gone missin'.

Bandulu found dis ransom note
And is de only clue.
Rastamouse, me need ya help,
Me nah know what to do!"

Rastamouse says, "Irie man,
Just let me check dat note."
The crook's demands were crystal clear.
And this is what he wrote:

My name's Bagga T.
Bagga Trouble, double G.
Me get dem babies to follow me.

Dem like da hip-hop vibes,
Riddim wicked, riddim live.
Me get dem orphans hip-hop-notized.

Me want bag-a C.
Bag-a cash, twenty G's.
If you want dem orphans to be set free.

Me want bag-a bling.
Bag-a stuff, bag-a ting.
Me want to get a ride dat fit for a king.

So leave da twenty G's,
In da woods, by da trees,
And don't let nobody come follow me...

Signed

Bagga T.

Rastamouse is well impressed,
"Man, dis bredda can really rap.
Let we go along with his greedy plan,
Keep watch and set up a trap."

So Rastamouse collects the cash,
Goes home to grate some cheese,
Then heads off to meet the Easy Crew
Who're waiting by the trees.

Next they hide and wait and watch,
And wait and watch until,
Scratchy Ranks gets sleepy
And Zoomer can't keep still.

"Dis waiting ting is boring,"
Zoomer says, then starts to play.
And while the Crew are watching him,
Bagga Trouble slips away.

Rastamouse says, "Him nah get far,
Dat orphan-teefin' mouse.
Me put someting extra in him bag
That will lead we to him house.

Me fix up da bag with a likkle hole
And put in some grated cheese.
So let's just look for the criminal's trail.
Easy Crew, follow me please."

Scratchy spots the cheesy trail
Which leads them to a store,
Where Rastamouse steps inside to ask,
The Manager if he saw . . .

To CRISS Trainer Shop

. . . the one who left the line of cheese
That's sprinkled on the floor:
"Because me have reason to believe
Dat mouse, him break da law."

The Manager says, "Yeah, a mouse came in,
Rapping to a hip-hop beat,
Paid in cash for some criss-looking trainers,
And then left with them on his feet."

Zoomer shouts, "Yo, Easy Crew,
Come see what I have found."
As he inspects some footprints
That he's noticed on the ground.

The Crew pursue the villain's prints
Which end up at 'Fat's 4 by 4'.
So Zoomer asks the salesman
If Bagga T was here before.

"Yes, he was here," the salesman began,
"He bought the latest jeep.
He paid in cash from a big money sack,
And you know dem jeep ain't cheap!"

The Crew pick up the tyre-track trail
And follow it quickly until,
It comes to a stop and disappears,
At the bottom of Natty Hill.

"It's a mystery," puzzles Scratchy,
"How come dem track jus' stop? –
But wait, I hear an irie sound,
Some real fly, rough, hip-hop."

Scratchy calls, "Come help me here,
I tink I found Bagga T."
So the Easy Crew push back the rock
And this is what they see:

A crowd of happy orphan mice
Hip-hopping in the place.
Screaming out for Bagga T
And rocking to the bass.

Rastamouse takes up the mike
And questions Bagga T:
"Why ya teef all dat money
Den not set dem orphans free?"

Rastamouse listens carefully
To Bagga T's wicked rhyme.
He sees deep down Bagga's heart is good
And that he's not cut out for crime.

So our hero says, "You broke da law,
And you have to pay da price.
You mus' hand back da cash and da bling and ting
And take back dem baby mice.

Da Easy Crew will escort you –
Make sure everyting get fix.
While I, Mouse, make an important call
Den we'll meet at da orphanage at six."

So Rastamouse calls the President
And asks him to agree
To a plan that will please the orphans
And fix up the crook, Bagga T.

When they meet at six, Bandulu says,
"All dem baby mice been fed.
Dem washed and inna dem pyjamas
But me jus' cyant get dem to bed."

Rastamouse turns to Bagga T:
"Now dis how ya pay for ya crime,
Ya gonna settle dem orphans down each night
With a rap at storytime.

And tonight once dem babies are fast asleep,
Me need ya to come with me.
There's someting missin' from da Easy Crew mix
And me sure it's your vibes, Bagga T."

So later that night at the studio,
When the tune is nearly done,
Bagga T raps on the final cut,
And in Mouseland, it reach Number One!

RiDE-Da-RiDDim

EASY CREW

featuring

Bagga Trouble

NUFF SONG

RIDE-DA-RIDDIM
Easy Crew
feat. Bagga Trouble

NO.1

"Easy Crew! Come in! Come in!
Are you reading me?
Message from the President,
Listen up you three!

Rastamouse! Come in! Come in!
Me loved ya wicked plan.
And ya tune is extra crucial,
Or as you would say, 'IRIE MAN'."

IRIE

pronounced: i-ree

anything positive or good

BLING

pronounced: bling

expensive, shiny jewellery

CRISS

pronounced: kris

very smart, the best

G's

pronounced: jeez

thousands or grands
(money)